BASKETBALL
Super Stars

By
David Gowdey

Illustrated by
Sam Whitehead

This book Belongs to

Grosset & Dunlap • New York

**AN
MBKA
PRODUCTION**

Copyright © 1994 by MBKA, Inc. All rights reserved.
Published by Grosset & Dunlap, Inc., a member of The
Putnam & Grosset Group, New York. GROSSET &
DUNLAP is a trademark of Grosset & Dunlap, Inc.
Published simultaneously in Canada. Printed in the U.S.A.
Library of Congress Catalog Card Number: 93-77476.
ISBN 0-448-40542-3
A B C D E F G H I J

THE SUPER STARS

Great athletes are often great entertainers, and nowhere is this more true than in basketball. The players gathered together in this book are among the most recognizable faces in America. Michael Jordan soars to new heights every night and astonishes the world with his inventiveness, while Charles Barkley, Patrick Ewing, and David Robinson have become America's most visible embodiments of drive and determination on the court. The long rivalry between two legends of the game, Larry Bird and Magic Johnson, lifted the NBA to new levels of popularity and today stands as a consummate example of grace and gallantry under pressure.

Now the sensational Shaquille O'Neal bursts upon the scene and challenges for a place beside the others in basketball's pantheon. Here's a behind-the-scenes look at seven of the greatest athletes in the world, men whose flair and masterful skills have helped redefine their sport.

Michael JORDAN

leapt forward and began to crowd him — the game was on the line! Michael was surrounded, but that was the idea. He looked to the right, then fired a pass against the flow to guard John Paxson, standing all alone in the left-hand corner. Swishh! The Bulls were champions at last!

Today Michael Jordan is at the top of his sport, and in many ways he transcends it.

Michael Jordan had been waiting a long time for this moment, and he didn't intend to fall short. It was game five of the 1991 NBA finals. With just a minute left, his team, the Chicago Bulls, led the L.A. Lakers, 103–101.

After years of close losses and early exits, the Bulls were close to a title. During the 1990–91 season Michael had dominated the game, but the Bulls had been labeled a one-man team. Could a one-man team win it all?

Michael brought the ball upcourt. He glanced to his right, then dribbled to the left side, which was closer to the basket. Suddenly he shifted his weight and cut right again, back across the court. The Lakers

One journalist has suggested that the only thing left for him to do is run for president. But politics can wait — for now he's the greatest player of the NBA's golden era.

Michael was born in Brooklyn, New York, on February 17, 1963, but he grew up in Wilmington, North Carolina, a quiet town on the ocean. His father worked at an electric plant, his mother at a bank. The Jordans didn't have a lot of money, but they were comfortable. His mother taught him to cook and sew, and Michael felt close to his family.

Michael started playing basketball at age 12. A basketball career seemed unlikely — he was only 5′9″, and no one in his family was over 6 feet. His older brother Larry, a varsity player, was only 5′9″. But Larry could dunk a basketball, a feat that inspired Michael to put in hours of hard practice.

THAT'S MY BRO!

When he won a place on an organized team, Michael chose number 23. His brother had been number 45, and Michael said he wanted to be at least half as good.

Michael's father put two hoops in the backyard, and Michael wore all the grass off the lawn. Neighborhood games lasted at least two hours a day, and all day on Saturdays. When he entered high school he was too small for the varsity team and was cut, but he excelled with the junior varsity, averaging 27 points a game.

Michael spent all his time on the court and neglected his schoolwork. His father told him that there was no way he could make it to college the way he was going. Michael saw he was right and soon began to concentrate on his studies.

Michael still has a habit he picked up from his father. It's an expression that's been caught in thousands of photos since he entered the NBA. When he's really concentrating, he sticks his tongue out on one side of his mouth. Michael saw his father do the same thing when he was working hard.

Although he no longer spent all day playing basketball, Michael began practicing harder than anyone on the team. When the two-hour junior practice ended, Michael would stay and practice with the varsity. A school official who'd graduated from the University of North Carolina eventually took notice and mentioned him to UNC coach Dean Smith. Michael was invited to the Five-Star summer basketball camp, where he spent three weeks with the best high-school players in the country.

Michael was shy at first, but soon got over it. In his first week at Five-Star camp he won five trophies, including MVP. Today he calls the camp "the turning point in my life."

Basketball scholarship offers began to pour in. Michael chose UNC, although he'd always rooted against them. He liked the campus, and he knew that Coach Dean Smith put a priority on seeing his Tar Heel players graduate.

In his first practice Michael dunked over a 7-foot center, surprising even himself. Soon Coach Smith named him a starter. ''He pays attention,'' said Smith. ''You tell him something and he does it.''

Michael maintained a B average while pacing UNC to the NCAA tournament. The Tar Heels made the 1982 final against Georgetown, and as a freshman guard, Michael finished off a remarkable year with a winning jump shot in the final seconds.

Over the summer Michael worked on his defense and returned to UNC a complete player. His tight defense led to more steals and blocks, and it helped the U.S. national team win a gold medal at the 1983 Pan Am Games. Although he decided to turn pro, Michael felt that basketball shouldn't be his whole life and returned to UNC over the next two summers to complete his degree.

The Bulls picked Michael third overall, behind centers Akeem Olajuwon and Sam Bowie. In the summer of 1984, before he joined the Bulls, he played under Bobby Knight for the U.S. gold medal Olympic team. Knight, he says, helped his concentration. At those Olympic Games, the world saw a superstar in the making.

In his first NBA season Michael made a convincing case that a superstar had already arrived, averaging over 28 points and playing superb defense. But there were those who said that the rookie didn't deserve the attention he received. At the 1985 All-Star Game, Michael noticed that he was being ignored on offense — no one would pass him the ball.

In the slam dunk contest the day before, Michael had called attention to himself by wearing a warm-up suit from his own line of sportswear, while the other players wore regular team gear. His mistake in judgment led to his being labeled a "show-off" for some time afterward, but the "freeze-out" didn't prevent him from being named Rookie of the Year. The Bulls made the playoffs and took a playoff game from Milwaukee before bowing out.

But the next year began with a setback. In the third game Michael broke a bone in his foot, and the team quickly lost eight of nine games. Healing was slow, and Michael sat on the sidelines, his foot in a cast. He was more frustrated than he'd ever been in his life. Against doctors' orders he began to play pickup games, explaining, "They haven't experienced the game like I have. I love it like a wife or a girlfriend."

Michael returned in March 1986, and although his playing time was limited, he carried the team into the playoffs. Against the Boston Celtics in the first round, he scored 49 points in the opening game, 30 in the first half. In game two, with the Bulls 2 points down, he stole the ball from Robert Parrish with 9 seconds left, then sank 2 free throws with no time on the clock. The teams battled for two overtime periods. Michael played 53 of 58 minutes and scored 63 points, a playoff record.

Michael was MVP the next year. He averaged over 37 points a game and became the first player in history with more than 200 steals and 100 blocks in the same season. Despite his efforts, the Bulls were beaten in the playoffs — only two teammates had been able to average as many as 9 points a game all year.

Trumpeter Wynton Marsalis once likened Michael to a great jazz soloist, inventing moves and twists never played before.

In 1989, Phil Jackson was named coach of the Bulls. Jackson knew that only one team had ever won the title with the league's leading scorer: the Milwaukee Bucks with Lew Alcindor (Kareem Abdul-Jabbar) in 1970–71. He decided he'd have to find a system under which the other Bulls would score more points. He stressed defense and instituted a college "triangle" offense, featuring quick passing and few play calls. The system bothered Michael at first, but it was better than playing one-on-five.

The new style worked. Michael continued his run of scoring titles, and the Bulls were better than they'd ever been. The Bulls pushed Detroit, the eventual champions, to the limit in the Central Division, and the next season blew past them in four games.

The second game of the 1991 finals featured one of Michael Jordan's greatest plays. In full flight on the fast break, he was rising toward the basket for a slam when he saw Laker Sam Perkins reaching up with his long arms. Caught in midair, Michael seemed to will himself higher, then switched the ball to his other hand and slammed it through. The Bulls didn't lose another game in that series.

Michael often seems to defy gravity, hanging in the air longer than other players. He has dunked with his eyes above the rim looking down, an incredible leap for a player who stands 6'6".

In 1992, Chicago faced a tough New York team in the seventh game of the NBA Eastern Conference finals.

Michael scored 29 points in the first half, 42 in the game, and the series was won.

The Bulls would defend their title in the finals against the Portland Trail Blazers. In game one, Portland started fast and took a 17–9 lead. Then Michael went to work. Elgin Baylor's championship series record of 33 points in a single half had stood for 30 years, but this night it would fall to Michael Jordan.

In a fantastic display of shooting, Michael hit 6 three-pointers on his way to a 35-point first half. After the sixth he turned to Magic Johnson, who was broadcasting the game courtside, and shrugged as if to say, "I don't believe it either." The Blazers held him scoreless for the first 3 minutes of the second half, but in those 3 minutes he collected 4 assists and the Bulls charged to victory.

Chicago led 3–2 in the series when they took the floor in Portland for the sixth game, but the last win wouldn't be easy. With their backs to the wall, the Trail Blazers played almost flawlessly and led, 79–64, after three quarters.

Michael was weary after playing 44 minutes in game five, and Coach Jackson took him out as the fourth quarter began. The game seemed lost, but the Bulls chipped away at the lead. Michael returned with less than 9 minutes to play, and combined with Scottie Pippen for the last 19 points down the stretch. The Bulls prevailed, 97–93, and won their second straight championship.

Michael Jordan led the Chicago Bulls to a third straight championship for the '92–'93 NBA season. He was also named MVP of the NBA Finals for the third consecutive year.

But in October of 1993, Michael shocked the sports world by announcing his retirement at the age of 30. His father had died tragically that summer, and Michael wanted to know that James Jordan had seen his last game. "I wanted to be remembered as a guy who enjoyed the game, always played it 110%," Michael explained. "I've reached the pinnacle of my career. I don't have anything else to prove."

MICHAEL JORDAN

COLLEGE RECORD

SEASON	TEAM	G	MIN	FG PCT	FT PCT	REB	PTS	AVG
81–82	North Carolina	34	—	.534	.722	149	460	13.5
82–83	North Carolina	36	—	.535	.737	197	721	20.0
83–84	North Carolina	31	—	.551	.779	163	607	19.6
TOTALS		101	—	.540	.748	509	1,788	17.7

NBA REGULAR SEASON RECORD

SEASON	TEAM	G	MIN	FG PCT	FT PCT	REB	AST	PTS	AVG
84–85	Chicago	82	3,144	.515	.845	534	481	2,313	28.2
85–86	Chicago	18	451	.457	.840	64	53	408	22.7
86–87	Chicago	82	3,281	.482	.857	430	377	3,041	37.1
87–88	Chicago	82	3,311	.535	.841	449	485	2,868	35.0
88–89	Chicago	81	3,255	.538	.850	652	650	2,633	32.5
89–90	Chicago	82	3,197	.526	.848	565	519	2,753	33.6
90–91	Chicago	82	3,034	.539	.851	492	453	2,580	31.5
91–92	Chicago	80	3,102	.519	.832	511	489	2,404	30.1
92–93	Chicago	78	3,067	.495	.837	522	428	2,541	32.6
TOTALS		667	25,842	.516	.846	4,219	3,935	21,541	32.3

NBA PLAYOFF RECORD

SEASON	TEAM	G	MIN	FG PCT	FT PCT	REB	AST	PTS	AVG
84–85	Chicago	4	171	.436	.828	23	34	117	29.3
85–86	Chicago	3	135	.505	.872	19	17	131	43.7
86–87	Chicago	3	128	.417	.897	21	18	107	35.7
87–88	Chicago	10	427	.531	.869	71	47	363	36.3
88–89	Chicago	17	718	.510	.799	119	130	591	34.8
89–90	Chicago	16	674	.514	.836	115	109	587	36.7
90–91	Chicago	17	689	.524	.845	108	142	529	31.1
91–92	Chicago	22	920	.499	.857	137	127	759	34.5
92–93	Chicago	19	783	.475	.805	128	114	666	35.1
TOTALS		111	4,645	.501	.834	741	738	3,850	34.7

NBA ALL-STAR GAME RECORD

SEASON	TEAM	MIN	FG PCT	FT PCT	REB	AST	PTS
1985	Chicago	22	.222	.750	6	2	7
1986	Chicago			Did not play — injured			
1987	Chicago	28	.417	.500	0	4	11
1988	Chicago	29	.739	1.000	8	3	40
1989	Chicago	33	.565	.500	2	3	28
1990	Chicago	29	.471	—	5	2	17
1991	Chicago	36	.400	.857	5	5	26
1992	Chicago	31	.529	—	1	5	18
1993	Chicago	36	.417	.692	4	5	30
TOTALS		244	.493	.750	31	29	177

MAGIC JOHNSON

One of the greatest basketball players of all time was born in Lansing, Michigan, on August 14, 1959. Earvin Johnson, Jr., grew up as one of ten children in a hardworking middle-class family. His father handled two full-time jobs: one as an autoworker, the other running a hauling service, taking away tree branches, refrigerators, and other trash. Magic helped his father with chores on weekends, often early Saturday morning after a win on the court the night before.

Magic had an after-school job, and earned extra money in the winter by shoveling snow for the neighborhood. "How could I refuse," he asks, "when my dad was working so hard?"

His father's example of hard work set a pattern for Magic's life that he has never forgotten. "I look for nothing from anyone," says Magic. "Whatever I want, I work for." Despite his reputation as a flamboyant player, the key to Magic's success is his unsurpassed grasp of the fundamentals — positional play, dribbling, passing, and shooting.

As a boy, Magic took a basketball with him wherever he went, dribbling on the sidewalk while balancing schoolbooks or groceries in his other hand.

Magic had a great career with Everett High School, winning the state championship in his senior year. In his sophomore year at Michigan State, Magic led the Spartans to a berth in the 1979 NCAA finals, where he faced Larry Bird and Indiana State, a team that was undefeated in 33 straight games. Both Bird and Magic had already attracted huge followings among college basketball fans, and when Magic led Michigan State to a 75-64 championship victory the stage was set for their arrival in the pros.

In many ways this single game changed the sport of basketball. The battle between the two college stars won a national spotlight, and the following season millions of college fans transferred allegiances over to the pros. In the 1980s the NBA became the hottest game in town, and the rivalry between Boston and Los Angeles, the league's two oldest franchises, reached a peak.

Ex–Lakers coach Pat Riley, now with the Knicks, once remarked that "Magic plays harder in practice than in the games," spurring his teammates on.

In the '80s Boston and Los Angeles met three times in the NBA finals, Magic and the Lakers winning twice. The Lakers made the finals eight times in the decade, and Larry still calls Magic "the best I've ever seen."

Magic brings tremendous enthusiasm for the game onto the court. On the opening night of his rookie year, 1979–80, Lakers veteran center Kareem Abdul-Jabbar sank a game-winning skyhook at the buzzer, and Magic shocked the unemotional superstar by leaping into his arms. All season Magic's presence charged up the team, and Los Angeles swept into the finals against the Philadelphia 76ers, who were led by Dr. J., Julius Erving.

The Lakers took a 3–2 lead in the series, but Kareem was injured in the fifth game in L.A. and couldn't make the trip back to Philadelphia. The rest of the team felt the loss keenly, and Magic noticed the team's sagging spirit. Ignoring established NBA traditions, the rookie decided to take charge. He symbolically sat in Kareem's seat during the flight back East.

When the game began, Magic lined up at *center* against the 76ers' Caldwell Jones, who was 3 inches taller. Magic leaped high to win the tap, took a quick return pass, then flew over the giant Darryl Dawkins for a lay-up.

Magic put everything he had into the sixth game, playing every position on the floor: point guard, shooting guard, small and power forward, and center. All night he evaded the NBA's greatest defenders, burying his jump shot from the outside or cruising in for a lay-up if the Sixers came out to him. He finished with 42 points,

16, 1980 game the most amazing of his career. "It's almost always in one or another of the VCRs in my house," he says, adding, "Whenever I'm down, I watch that game."

In his senior year in high school Magic had captained his team to the state championship, two years later he led

15 rebounds, 7 assists, and 3 steals. He shot 61 percent from the floor and made 15 of 15 free throws. It was one of the greatest performances in NBA history, and the Lakers were crowned champions while Kareem watched on TV, thousands of miles away. Magic still calls the May

Michigan State to the NCAA title, and now he'd driven the Lakers past the rest of the NBA. It was hard to see how he could go anywhere but down, yet Magic kept it up. He became the centerpiece of the Lakers' "Showtime" fast-break offense, running all the plays.

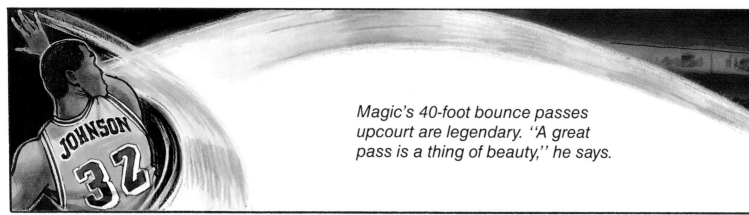

Magic's 40-foot bounce passes upcourt are legendary. "A great pass is a thing of beauty," he says.

...LIGHTS...CAMERA... ACTION!

Magic says that when he decided to become a great passer he had to "give up thinking like a scorer." He likens himself to the director of a movie instead of the star, coaxing the maximum performance out of his teammates.

The Lakers dominated the NBA in the 1980s, winning five finals and playing in eight championship series. Magic was an all-star player year after year and was voted NBA MVP three times.

Magic brings a special joy to every game and every practice. As he once put it, he has "a burning desire to be the very best player on the best team." His rivalry with Larry Bird was heated at times, but as they continued to meet they developed a respect for each other and became good friends.

SWISH!

Magic has always concentrated on every phase of his own game. His house includes a full-size basketball court, and when word circulated early in his career that he was too cautious about taking the outside shot, Magic went to work. He put in hundreds of hours on his home court and improved his shooting percentage. During his first five years in the league, his shooting got better every single year.

PRACTICE MAKES PERFECT

At home Magic can always be found on his court first thing in the morning, shooting hoops.

On November 7, 1991, the world of basketball was stunned to hear that Magic had contracted the AIDS virus and was retiring at age 32. His friends all over the world rallied around him as he set out to face his greatest challenge: increasing public awareness about the HIV virus and bringing people together to fight this disease.

Magic came back to the court for the All-Star Game and played magnificently. He scored 25 points, made 9 assists, and sank a three-pointer at the buzzer. U.S. coach Chuck Daly had no hesitation approving Magic for the American team at the

Magic's moving television special with young AIDS patients, "A Conversation With Magic," is being shown today in many countries.

1992 Barcelona Olympics, explaining, "We need his leadership." The Dream Team played the sport as it has never been played before, and Magic was the team's core.

The joy of playing the game he loved proved too much for Magic to resist. He announced he'd be returning to the NBA, signed a new contract, and averaged 10 points and 12 assists a game in the preseason.

But his comeback fell short. Although he didn't want to be treated differently from any other player, Magic was disturbed to hear that some opponents were reacting negatively and fearfully to his return. So he retired a final time before the season began. He knows he'll miss the game he loves, but he plans to concentrate all his efforts on raising public awareness about the HIV virus.

His wife, Cookie, and new baby have tested negative for the disease, and they remain a constant source of strength for Magic. In the past year, his continuing grace under tremendous stress and pressure has proven him a truly heroic figure. For millions of fans he stands taller than ever.

COLLEGE RECORD

SEASON	TEAM	G	MIN	FG PCT	FT PCT	REB	PTS	AVG
77–78	Michigan State	30	—	.458	.785	237	511	17
78–79	Michigan State	32	1159	.468	.842	234	548	17.1
TOTALS		62	—	.463	.816	471	1,059	17.1

NBA REGULAR SEASON RECORD

SEASON	TEAM	G	MIN	FG PCT	FT PCT	REB	AST	PTS	AVG
79–80	Los Angeles	77	2,795	.530	.810	596	563	1,387	18
80–81	Los Angeles	37	1,371	.532	.760	320	317	798	21.6
81–82	Los Angeles	78	2,991	.537	.760	751	743	1,447	18.6
82–83	Los Angeles	79	2,907	.548	.800	683	829	1,326	16.8
83–84	Los Angeles	67	2,567	.565	.810	491	875	1,178	17.6
84–85	L.A. Lakers	77	2,781	.561	.843	476	968	1,406	18.3
85–86	L.A. Lakers	72	2,578	.526	.871	426	907	1,354	18.8
86–87	L.A. Lakers	80	2,904	.522	.848	504	977	1,909	23.9
87–88	L.A. Lakers	72	2,637	.492	.853	449	858	1,408	19.6
88–89	L.A. Lakers	77	2,886	.509	.911	607	988	1,730	22.5
89–90	L.A. Lakers	79	2,937	.480	.890	522	907	1,765	22.3
90–91	L.A. Lakers	79	2,933	.477	.906	551	989	1,531	19.4
91–92	L.A. Lakers		Did not play						
TOTALS		874	32,287	.521	.848	6,376	9,921	17,239	19.7

NBA PLAYOFF RECORD

SEASON	TEAM	G	MIN	FG PCT	FT PCT	REB	AST	PTS	AVG
79–80	Los Angeles	16	658	.518	.802	168	151	293	18.3
80–81	Los Angeles	3	127	.388	.650	41	21	51	17.0
81–82	Los Angeles	14	562	.529	.828	158	130	243	17.4
82–83	Los Angeles	15	643	.485	.840	128	192	268	17.9
83–84	Los Angeles	21	837	.551	.800	139	284	382	18.2
84–85	L.A. Lakers	19	687	.513	.847	134	289	333	17.5
85–86	L.A. Lakers	14	541	.537	.766	100	211	302	21.6
86–87	L.A. Lakers	18	666	.539	.831	139	219	392	21.8
87–88	L.A. Lakers	24	965	.514	.852	130	303	477	19.9
88–89	L.A. Lakers	14	518	.489	.907	83	165	258	18.4
89–90	L.A. Lakers	9	376	.490	.886	57	115	227	25.2
90–91	L.A. Lakers	19	823	.440	.882	154	240	414	21.8
TOTALS		186	7,403	.508	.838	1,431	2,320	3,640	19.6

NBA ALL-STAR GAME RECORD

SEASON	TEAM	MIN	FG PCT	FT PCT	REB	AST	PTS
1980	Los Angeles	24	.625	1.000	2	4	12
1982	Los Angeles	23	.556	.857	4	7	16
1983	Los Angeles	33	.438	.750	5	16	17
1984	Los Angeles	37	.462	1.000	9	22	15
1985	L.A. Lakers	31	.500	.875	5	15	21
1986	L.A. Lakers	28	.333	1.000	4	15	6
1987	L.A. Lakers	34	.400	.500	7	13	9
1988	L.A. Lakers	39	.267	1.000	6	19	17
1989	L.A. Lakers		Did not play — injured				
1990	L.A. Lakers	25	.600	—	6	4	22
1991	L.A. Lakers	28	.438	—	4	3	16
1992	L.A. Lakers	29	.750	1.000	5	9	25
TOTALS		331	.489	.905	57	127	176

Patrick EWING

Patrick Ewing waited coolly while basketball commissioner David Stern welcomed an overflow crowd of fans and reporters to the NBA draft lottery. After the most charmed career in the history of college basketball, there was no doubt in anyone's mind that Patrick would be the number-one pick. But he still didn't know where he'd be going. All the teams that had missed the playoffs were eligible, and there were some less-than-great teams among them. Would Patrick end up with a good team? His future was at stake.

The crowd grew quiet as the choice was made: ''The New York Knicks!'' Patrick grinned. He'd be the main man on a team with a great tradition, in the media capital of the world. He was headed for the Big Apple, New York City.

The Knicks had fallen a long way from the glory years — the early 1970s. During those years, stars like Walt Frazier, Bill Bradley, and Willis Reed won NBA titles in some of the most dramatic games ever played. When seriously-injured center Reed left the hospital and started the seventh game of the 1970 finals against all the odds, his courage inspired a magnificent effort from teammates and they rallied to take the title. Since then no Knick center had been able to fill his shoes. And although it had once been one of the greats, the New York Knicks hadn't seen glory days in almost two decades.

Expectations for the 23-year-old rookie ran high. New York's tabloids ran front-page headlines. For someone who'd lived just eleven years in the U.S., all this attention would take some getting used to.

By high school Patrick was an outstanding player and a tremendous rebounder. He won championships at two different schools and was widely recruited, finally deciding on nearby Georgetown.

Patrick Ewing was born in Kingston, Jamaica, on August 5, 1962. In Jamaica, sports are still dominated by the game of cricket and its great West Indian stars. West Indies cricketers are more than sports heroes; they are also political forces. Patrick grew up in an environment where sports figures had to be not only first-class at their game, but dignified and impressive away from it, too.

Patrick's family moved to Washington, D.C., when he was 11 years old. Life was much more hectic here than in Jamaica, and it took Patrick a while to adjust. He took an interest in basketball immediately, and it wasn't long before people began to notice his skill.

Georgetown's John Thompson is regarded as a legendary college basketball coach, and Patrick did a lot to help his career. Thompson had once been a Boston Celtic, a spirited, emotional player beside such stars as Bill Russell and John Havlicek. With shrewdness and hard work he'd assembled a powerful team at Georgetown, but he needed a leader on the court. Patrick proved to be a leader and more.

Called "a warrior" by Coach Thompson, Patrick's serious, sometimes scowling demeanor on the court could intimidate opponents.

Patrick captained the Hoyas to the NCAA finals three times in his four college years and was tournament MVP in 1984. Georgetown had a record of 121–23 during Patrick's college career. And in his senior season he swept the major awards, including the Naismith Trophy and the Adolph Rupp Trophy as NCAA Player of the Year.

In the summer of 1984, Patrick played for Coach Thompson alongside Michael Jordan on the gold medal U.S. Olympic team.

Patrick was such a great player that the NBA changed the rules of its entry draft because of him. Until Patrick came along, the last-place team got the first draft pick. Now the bottom seven teams had their names drawn to determine the draft order. The new rule prevented teams that were low in the standings from deliberately losing in order to have the first pick: Patrick.

After the NBA lottery, Patrick's contract with the Knicks set another record, and expectations ran sky-high.

But it wouldn't be that easy. Once the 1985–86 season started, the 7-foot, 255-pound rookie let the team veterans control the game. "I didn't want them to think I got a big head because I made a lot of money," he explained. He was reserved off the court, and guarded in interviews. Coach Hubie Brown said that rookie centers rarely dominate right away, and moved Patrick to power forward beside Bill Cartwright at center.

The fans began to grow restless. Madison Square Garden fans had always rooted for Georgetown rival St. John's, who featured popular Brooklyn-born Chris Mullin. They'd booed the somber Patrick and the Hoyas before, and now they were proving hard to please.

In his first year Patrick missed 32 games because of injuries. During that season the Knicks won 23 games, one fewer than the year before. The next year they won 24 games. Despite the setbacks, Patrick averaged 20 points and 9 rebounds a game and was named Rookie of the Year. He maintained consistently good numbers and became more confident over the next two years.

Always a strong force "in the paint," Patrick's favorite shot is a deadly turnaround jumper.

It was in his third season, 1987–88, that Patrick really came into his own. New coach Rick Pitino drew up an aggressive full-court press defense to force mistakes by the other team. When the year began, he opened up the offense and dropped some of the veterans. Patrick finally felt at home in the NBA. He knew what he had to do to win. And he was tired of losing.

That year he led the Knicks into the playoffs with a tremendous late charge, averaging 26 points and 10 rebounds down the stretch. He began to use his great speed as the Knicks' offense opened up, and he found a real asset in point guard Mark Jackson. His hesitation was gone — every part of his game was swift and sure. He added some moves under the basket, including a new jump hook shot that kept opponents off balance.

Since then, Patrick has shattered Richie Guerin's club record of 2,347 points. He holds the Knicks' record for blocked shots and is consistently among league leaders in rebounds, scoring, blocks, and field-goal percentage.

Off the court Patrick has grown more relaxed and assured. Patrick's a genuinely funny and likable man who's down to earth. He's been called a "lunch-pail superstar," a man who never takes himself too seriously. But in the tremendous 1992 NBA quarterfinal series against the defending champion Chicago Bulls, he rose to new heights.

Patrick had been bothered by a bad ankle in games four and five of the series, but he came back to dominate game six. Under the national spotlight, he shook off double-teaming defenders with his intelligent passing and sank shot after shot from all over the floor.

In the most physical game of the 1992 playoffs, Patrick finished with 27 points, forcing the series to a seventh game.

Longtime New York fans were reminded of Willis Reed's inspirational championship performance, a Knicks moment that until then had never been approached. Although the Bulls went on to win game seven in Chicago, Patrick had given reason to believe that his best was still yet to come.

PATRICK EWING

COLLEGE RECORD

SEASON	TEAM	G	MIN	FG PCT	FT PCT	REB	PTS	AVG
81–82	Georgetown	37	1,064	.631	.617	279	469	12.7
82–83	Georgetown	32	1,024	.570	.629	325	565	17.7
83–84	Georgetown	37	1,179	.658	.656	371	608	16.4
84–85	Georgetown	37	1,132	.625	.638	341	542	14.6
TOTALS		143	4,399	.620	.635	1,316	2,184	15.3

NBA REGULAR SEASON RECORD

SEASON	TEAM	G	MIN	FG PCT	FT PCT	REB	AST	PTS	AVG
85–86	New York	50	1,771	.474	.739	451	102	998	20.0
86–87	New York	63	2,206	.503	.713	555	104	1,356	21.5
87–88	New York	82	2,546	.555	.716	676	125	1,653	20.2
88–89	New York	80	2,896	.567	.746	740	188	1,815	22.7
89–90	New York	82	3,165	.551	.775	893	182	2,347	28.6
90–91	New York	81	3,104	.514	.745	905	244	2,154	26.6
91–92	New York	82	3,150	.522	.738	921	156	1,970	24.0
92–93	New York	81	3,003	.503	.719	980	151	1,959	24.2
TOTALS		601	21,841	.526	.738	6,121	1,252	14,252	23.7

NBA PLAYOFF RECORD

SEASON	TEAM	G	MIN	FG PCT	FT PCT	REB	AST	PTS	AVG
87–88	New York	4	153	.491	.864	51	10	75	18.8
88–89	New York	9	340	.486	.750	90	20	179	19.9
89–90	New York	10	395	.521	.823	105	31	294	29.4
90–91	New York	3	110	.400	.778	30	6	50	16.7
91–92	New York	12	482	.456	.740	133	27	272	22.7
92–93	New York	15	605	.512	.638	164	36	382	25.5
TOTALS		53	2,085	.491	.747	573	130	1,252	23.6

NBA ALL-STAR GAME RECORD

SEASON	TEAM	MIN	FG PCT	FT PCT	REB	AST	PTS
1986	New York		Did not play — injured				
1988	New York	16	.500	1.000	6	0	9
1989	New York	17	.250	0.000	6	2	4
1990	New York	27	.556	1.000	10	1	12
1991	New York	30	.800	1.000	10	0	18
1992	New York	17	.571	.400	4	0	10
1993	New York	25	.636	1.000	10	1	15
TOTALS		132	.566	.533	.46	4	68

SHAQ

The game wasn't especially important. It was early in the season, and two teams in the middle of the pack, Golden State and Orlando, were running the floor and trading baskets. An Orlando Magic player lost possession, and the ball headed out of bounds. Then suddenly the crowd was electrified. The biggest man on the floor — over 7 feet tall, 300 pounds — was racing after it as hard as he could.

The ball was flying toward the line, but the player dove, fully extended, and caught it in midair! He crashed to the floor, and slid toward the sideline, 15 feet away. He wanted to pass, but there was no teammate nearby. He considered calling time-out, but there was no referee in sight. So Shaquille O'Neal did the only thing he could do to keep the ball in play. Just as he crossed the boundary he threw the ball high in the air. A moment later he crashed into a row of court-side photographers, a big grin on his face. The "Shaq" had arrived!

Often double-teamed, Shaquille O'Neal plays hard every moment he's on the court and draws more than his share of rough fouls. But a foul that would anger many players seldom seems to bother Shaquille. He actually seems to chuckle to himself at the crude attempt to slow him down, then goes out and beats his opponent to the next ball. Rick Mahorn of the New Jersey Nets admits he's grateful that Shaq's not a mean player: "If Shaq ever got mean, there wouldn't be a league."

Shaq was raised in Newark, New Jersey. His father was an army sergeant, and Shaq absorbed much of the older man's sense of order and discipline. But he's as fun-loving as any player in the NBA, and loves to "mug" for the camera.

Pro scouts had been keeping an eye on Shaquille since his days in high school, and he was drafted as a college under-classman. By mid-season of his rookie year Shaq was averaging 23.7 points a game with 14.5 rebounds and 4 blocks. In 1993, at the age of 20, he was voted to start the All-Star Game for the East ahead of superstar Patrick Ewing. But he didn't let the honors go to his head. "Pat's a great player," said Shaq. "I'm a pretty good player."

Shaquille O'Neal was underestimating himself. No one since Larry Bird or Magic Johnson has risen so quickly to the heights of the game, and no one in the NBA has as bright a future. Some nights he may come out second best to a Ewing or a Robinson, but, says Shaq, "I'll always come back. That's what's great about America. There's always a sequel."

After averaging 23.4 points a game and finishing second in the league in rebounding, Shaquille crowned a fantastic debut season by winning 96 of a possible 98 votes for NBA Rookie of the Year.

Shaquille's huge frame, shaved head, and full-length black leather coats with the Superman logo on the back make him a "walking photo-op."

Charles BARKLEY

Larry Bird's legendary career ended in the summer of 1992, and several players are trying to take Bird's place as basketball's greatest forward. Karl Malone of the Utah Jazz is one player who's often mentioned. But the consensus winner is Charles Barkley. He's been known to make some brash statements — like telling Bird as a rookie that he'd be his ''worst nightmare for the next ten years'' — but no one in the game can back those statements up like Charles.

At 6'4" Charles is one of the shortest NBA forwards in many years, but he's also one of the most effective. He uses every ounce of his 255 pounds under the basket, jostling for position. When he was once asked about his technique for winning rebounds, he grinned and said, ''My technique is simple — just go get the ball!''

In college, Charles's shape led a local reporter to dub him "The Round Mound of Rebound," but in the course of his career he's turned it into "Sir Charles."

Charles was born February 20, 1963, in Leeds, Alabama, a poverty-ridden town in the heart of the South. During the 1960s, the civil rights movement was just starting to change the way people thought about African Americans in America.

Charles was raised by his mother and grandmother. The family struggled, but there was always plenty of love and support.

Charles was heavyset growing up, and gave little thought to being a pro athlete. But even though he didn't make the varsity team in high school, his grandmother wouldn't let him give up on sports. Uncertain at first about his skills, Charles would wait until other kids had left the playground, then shoot baskets by himself at night.

The summer before he entered eleventh grade, Charles grew to be almost 6 feet tall. He began working and playing with total dedication. He knew that at his height he'd have to work on his leap, so he got ahold of a skipping rope and jumped rope for hours on end.

Charles has been dogged by controversy from the beginning of his career. He heard racist remarks from both blacks and whites while attending a high school that had mostly white students. Although the varsity coach was black, he kept Charles off the varsity team at first.

According to Charles's grandmother, this was because ''he'd only been playing with the white boys.''

Charles worried his grandmother with his habit of jumping the 42-inch chain-link fence around his house from a standing start. Sometimes he jumped the fence all afternoon, going back and forth like a jumping jack.

Charles made huge strides every season. His shooting wasn't very strong at first, but his tremendous rebounding impressed college recruiters. He chose to attend Auburn in the Southeast Conference, and led the conference in rebounding every year he played. The school made the most of their "Round Mound," publicizing his eating habits off the court as much as his amazing playing on it. He played strongly at the 1984 Olympic Trials, and although he was cut, he impressed the pro scouts and was drafted that spring.

"All racists need to feel secure about themselves," Charles says. *"So they get mad at somebody who's not like them, instead of facing the truth — that they're losers."*

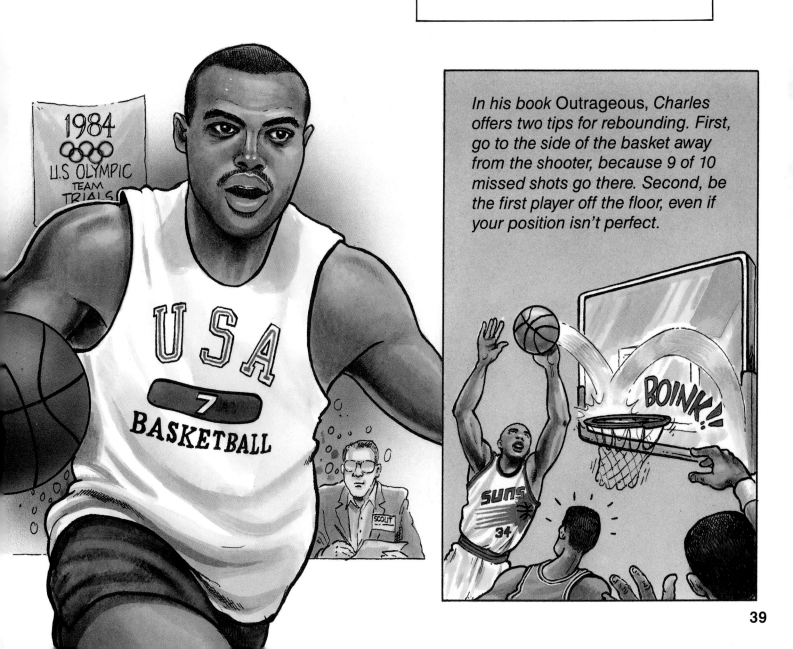

In his book Outrageous, *Charles offers two tips for rebounding. First, go to the side of the basket away from the shooter, because 9 of 10 missed shots go there. Second, be the first player off the floor, even if your position isn't perfect.*

It's often said that no player in the NBA does as many things as well as Charles Barkley. He began with the Philadelphia 76ers as a guard, and today he's the quickest forward in basketball. He's also the league's shortest forward, but his height doesn't hinder his game. Charles can leap as high as anyone, and he's completely fearless. He often blocks the lane like a football linebacker, putting his body on the line against much bigger players.

Charles loves to break a game open by going the length of the floor, charging upcourt with his barely-in-control, high-bounce dribble. He splits the defenders, soars to the basket, and rams the ball through the hoop. Then he sways from the rim in midair, rocking back and forth while he savors the moment.

Charles's willingness to hassle a team-mate who isn't giving 100 percent led to some disarray in the 76ers' locker room. But he thinks it's justified if the words lead to a personnel shake-up, or an improvement in play. "I believe in expressing what you feel," says Charles. But not everyone in the league agrees with that.

Charles remains one of the league's most controversial players, always willing to speak out on a variety of subjects. He describes how he ignored peer pressure to do drugs as a youngster and fought off racist attacks in college. He has confronted unruly fans in the arenas and bitter charges in the media. But sometimes his quotes land him in trouble, and during the Dream Team's appearance at the Olympics he was accused of insulting teams from other countries.

Like everyone in the NBA, Charles has great respect for Magic Johnson, and during the 1992 season he changed his own number to Magic's 32 in tribute.

They talked about their families and discovered they had much in common. But becoming friendly off the court hasn't changed their playing one bit.

Despite his feelings for Magic, Charles insists that athletes shouldn't be considered role models. Having been without a father in his own home as a boy, he tells young fans that their fathers, not Charles Barkley, are the real heroes. Men who work and make sacrifices for their families are the people who should be most admired. Charles tries to bring black businessmen with him when he speaks to youth groups, because he wants to show that there are many ways to reach goals besides playing basketball.

Charles has long-standing feuds with several of the NBA's rougher players, most noticeably the Detroit Pistons' Bill Laimbeer. He and Laimbeer got into a big fight when Charles saw the Piston center trying to intimidate 76er Rick Mahorn in a rough game. The league fined and suspended him, and Charles had to pay over $51,000 for the fight. But Charles claimed it was worth it to back up a teammate.

Later Charles and Laimbeer appeared in a film together, and to their surprise the two enjoyed each other's company.

Charles knows firsthand how hard it is to reach the NBA. When approached by a boy who dreams of glory in the pros, Charles reminds him how few of the thousands of college players actually make it, even for one season. There are only 324 players in the league at one time, and about 50 new spots a year.

Charles strongly believes that a good education must come first, along with the discipline to carve out a career. He once wrote that "If there should be any pressure on young athletes, it should be that they get an education, that they obtain a degree and focus their energy on becoming productive citizens in any number of professions." As far as making the NBA goes, he says that most people have "a better chance of landing on the moon."

Nevertheless, some make it, and Charles Barkley has made it big. In the course of his eight-year career he has averaged over 23 points and 11 rebounds a game. He led the NBA in rebounds in 1987 and was the All-Star Game MVP in 1991.

Although he'd been injured for several weeks before the All-Star Game, Charles kept playing to help keep the 76ers in the playoff picture, expecting to take a few days off at the midseason break. But the league office threatened him with a suspension if he didn't play in the All-Star Game after being chosen — after all, they said, he'd been playing every night.

On a badly swollen, fractured ankle, Charles gave an inspired performance, grabbing 22 rebounds and scoring 17 points to win an unusually physical game. Charles's 22 rebounds were the most in the All-Star Game in twenty-four years.

Playing well in the All-Star Game went against the odds, but Charles Barkley has been beating the odds for as long as anyone can remember. And that's just what to expect from this great player in the future!

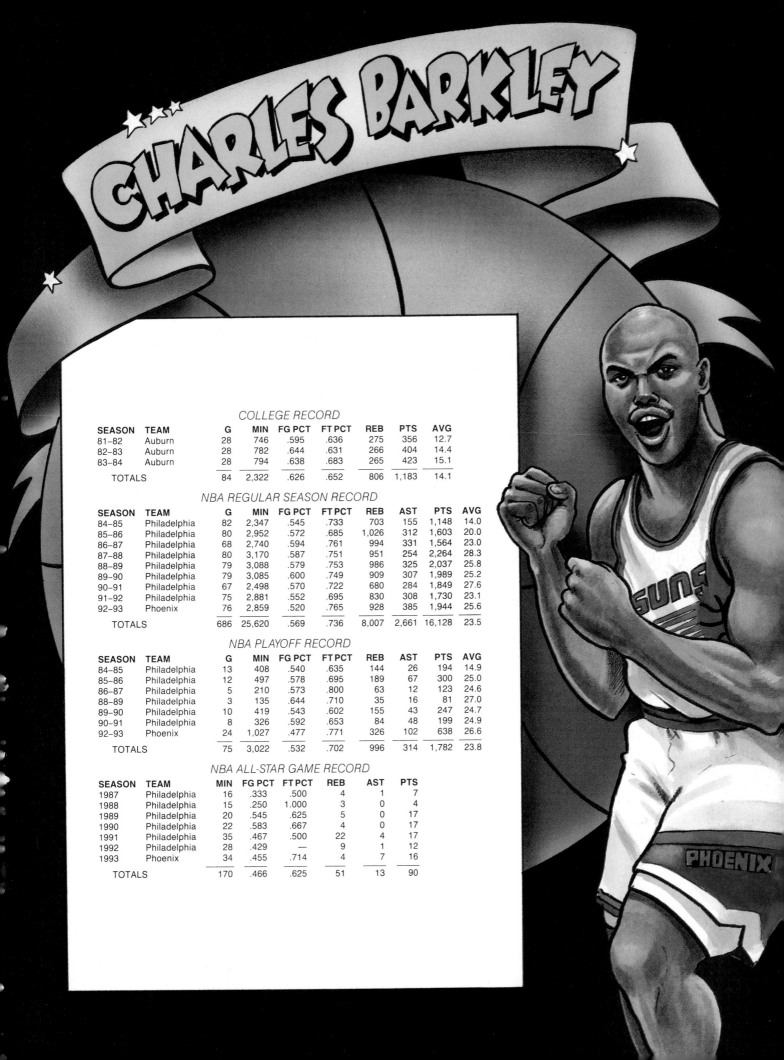

CHARLES BARKLEY

COLLEGE RECORD

SEASON	TEAM	G	MIN	FG PCT	FT PCT	REB	PTS	AVG
81–82	Auburn	28	746	.595	.636	275	356	12.7
82–83	Auburn	28	782	.644	.631	266	404	14.4
83–84	Auburn	28	794	.638	.683	265	423	15.1
TOTALS		84	2,322	.626	.652	806	1,183	14.1

NBA REGULAR SEASON RECORD

SEASON	TEAM	G	MIN	FG PCT	FT PCT	REB	AST	PTS	AVG
84–85	Philadelphia	82	2,347	.545	.733	703	155	1,148	14.0
85–86	Philadelphia	80	2,952	.572	.685	1,026	312	1,603	20.0
86–87	Philadelphia	68	2,740	.594	.761	994	331	1,564	23.0
87–88	Philadelphia	80	3,170	.587	.751	951	254	2,264	28.3
88–89	Philadelphia	79	3,088	.579	.753	986	325	2,037	25.8
89–90	Philadelphia	79	3,085	.600	.749	909	307	1,989	25.2
90–91	Philadelphia	67	2,498	.570	.722	680	284	1,849	27.6
91–92	Philadelphia	75	2,881	.552	.695	830	308	1,730	23.1
92–93	Phoenix	76	2,859	.520	.765	928	385	1,944	25.6
TOTALS		686	25,620	.569	.736	8,007	2,661	16,128	23.5

NBA PLAYOFF RECORD

SEASON	TEAM	G	MIN	FG PCT	FT PCT	REB	AST	PTS	AVG
84–85	Philadelphia	13	408	.540	.635	144	26	194	14.9
85–86	Philadelphia	12	497	.578	.695	189	67	300	25.0
86–87	Philadelphia	5	210	.573	.800	63	12	123	24.6
88–89	Philadelphia	3	135	.644	.710	35	16	81	27.0
89–90	Philadelphia	10	419	.543	.602	155	43	247	24.7
90–91	Philadelphia	8	326	.592	.653	84	48	199	24.9
92–93	Phoenix	24	1,027	.477	.771	326	102	638	26.6
TOTALS		75	3,022	.532	.702	996	314	1,782	23.8

NBA ALL-STAR GAME RECORD

SEASON	TEAM	MIN	FG PCT	FT PCT	REB	AST	PTS
1987	Philadelphia	16	.333	.500	4	1	7
1988	Philadelphia	15	.250	1.000	3	0	4
1989	Philadelphia	20	.545	.625	5	0	17
1990	Philadelphia	22	.583	.667	4	0	17
1991	Philadelphia	35	.467	.500	22	4	17
1992	Philadelphia	28	.429	—	9	1	12
1993	Phoenix	34	.455	.714	4	7	16
TOTALS		170	.466	.625	51	13	90

Larry BIRD

Larry Bird was born in West Baden, Indiana, on December 3, 1956. Indiana is a state where high school basketball games often receive front-page coverage in the newspapers. His older brother, Mark, was a good player and let Larry sit with him on the team bus going home from games. But as a boy Larry never imagined playing basketball for a living. He wasn't fast and couldn't jump very high: his favorite sport wasn't basketball, but baseball.

Larry made the second, or "B," basketball team as a freshman in high school. Although he sat on the bench for most of the games, his coach encouraged him to learn the fundamentals: how to pivot, how to establish position for rebounds, and how to dribble with his left hand.

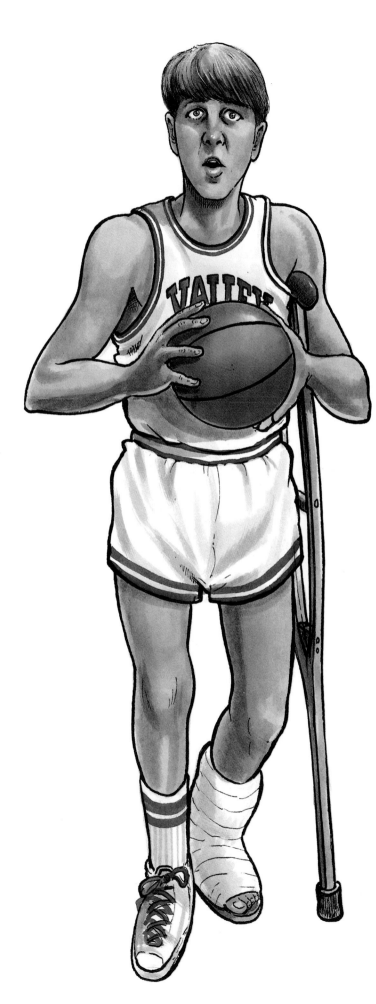

In his sophomore year, Larry broke his ankle in a game and missed most of the rest of the season. He made the most of his time off. Every day he would lean on a crutch and shoot as many free throws as he could. As soon as he was used to walking with the crutch, he began to play again. He wasn't really able to shoot, but his immobility made him concentrate on fakes and deception, and it changed his approach to passing. He started to see a whole new dimension in the game.

At the end of that season, Larry came back to play in the local high school tournament final, and sank 2 free throws in the final moments to win the game.

From then on, Larry Bird was committed to basketball. He'd play every morning from 6 A.M. until school began, and would shoot between classes if he could sneak into the gym. His home life wasn't always easy, because his father changed jobs a lot, but Larry felt as if he'd found his place on the court.

Larry can write with both hands, and he became so adept at dribbling with his left hand that he's just as strong passing an opponent on either side.

Larry grew to be 6′9″, and after high school he attended Indiana University for a semester. He played under famed coach Bobby Knight, but his small-town background hadn't prepared him for a big university. He felt lost.

When Larry's parents got divorced, he had a hard time. He left Indiana to make some money in a blue-collar job, planning to return later. He married a young woman he'd known only a short time, but the marriage didn't work out. Shortly afterward his father, depressed about many things, took his own life. It was the darkest time of Larry's life, yet he didn't allow it to get the best of him. On the basketball court he found a way to work through his troubles, and in time he got better and better.

Larry returned to school, this time Indiana State, and joined the basketball team. Because he'd transferred he wasn't allowed to play for a year, but he suited up with the rest of the team and played with the second unit in practice. After a while his group began to outplay the first team day after day. After a few weeks, his coach insisted the newcomer sit on the bench during the practice games. When Larry protested, the coach explained he was making the first team look so bad that they were losing all their confidence!

In his first year of actual play, Larry made third-team All-America. With good coaching he learned the fine points of playing defense and took over the leadership of the team. In a game against Bradley College, the opposing coach put three defenders on Larry, leaving only two Bradley

In the second half of the 1979 NCAA semifinal against DePaul, Larry hit 10 straight shots from the field.

players to guard the other four Indiana State players. Larry scored only 4 points, but his teammates ran wild and turned the game into a rout.

The twelve players who played on the Indiana State team grew close, and in 1979, Larry's senior year, he paced them to the NCAA tournament. His teammates weren't exceptional players, but Larry wouldn't let them lose.

Playing a tight man-to-man defense and helping each other out, Indiana State reached the final game. They were up against a very talented Michigan State team that included Magic Johnson. The game was close, but Michigan State's zone defense and Magic's superb work on the fast break sealed their fate. Michigan State won, 75–64.

After opposing each other in that classic final, Magic Johnson and Larry Bird entered the NBA together. In the next years they brought the sport up to a new level, one where passing and spontaneity are as important as strength and speed. Their dedicated team play and creativity on the court won millions of new fans for the game.

Larry joined the Boston Celtics in 1979–80, and the team climbed from 29 wins the year before to 61, an NBA-record improvement. Larry won the MVP award three years in a row and was all-NBA in each of his first nine seasons.

Larry was always at his best in the clutch. While leading the Celtics to five finals and three championships in the '80s, he became the team's all-time leading playoff scorer.

Larry is a great three-point shooter. He entered the NBA the year the three-point shot was adopted, and for a time thought little about this kind of shooting. But since he was such an accurate shooter, his percentage was good: during the 1985–86 season he made 25 of 34 shots in one stretch. He knew that a successful three-pointer often deflates the other team, and as the years went by he made it a big part of his game. One of Larry's favorite times to use the shot was directly off an inbound pass, when he wasn't covered quite as closely as in the heat of the game. Kevin McHale fired the ball to a prearranged point and Larry put it up right away.

Larry won the three-point shooting contest before the All-Star Game the first three years it was held. His favorite place to take the shot was from the corner, where it isn't quite as long. From here he always used a standing set shot, and made sure his feet were together.

In the 1990–91 season, Larry suffered a serious back injury and missed 22 games. He returned from surgery in 1991–92, but it was clear that his back still bothered him.

At the end of the 1991–92 season, Larry was picked to represent the United States at the Summer Olympics in Barcelona. The back injury still hampered his play, but choosing a Dream Team without Larry Bird was unthinkable.

Larry was the Celtics' best defensive rebounder, and their running game suffered when they didn't have him firing the ball upcourt.

In Barcelona, players from all over the world crowded around him before and after the games. They all wanted to have their picture taken with him, shake his hand, and tell him how much they admired him. The U.S. team dominated the tournament, and Larry won an Olympic gold medal to add to his other awards. It was a fitting end to a great career, and soon afterward he announced his retirement.

Larry Bird scored over 20,000 points in his career, but he will be remembered best for his brilliant passing and his exemplary leadership. Long one of the league's "greats," Larry was the ultimate team player in many ways. As he puts it, he "loves to see the gleam in a team-mate's eyes."

"Players will see right through a phony," Larry said once, "and they can tell when you're not giving it all you've got. Leadership is diving for a loose ball, getting the crowd involved, and getting other players involved — no more, no less."

LARRY BIRD

COLLEGE RECORD

SEASON	TEAM	G	MIN	FG PCT	FT PCT	REB	PTS	AVG
74–75	Indiana			Did not play				
75–76	Indiana State			Did not play				
76–77	Indiana State	28	1,033	.544	.840	373	918	32.8
77–78	Indiana State	32	—	.524	.793	369	959	30.0
78–79	Indiana State	34	—	.532	.831	505	973	28.6
TOTALS		94	—	.533	.822	1,247	2,850	30.3

NBA REGULAR SEASON RECORD

SEASON	TEAM	G	MIN	FG PCT	FT PCT	REB	AST	PTS	AVG
79–80	Boston	82	2,955	.474	.836	852	370	1,745	21.3
80–81	Boston	82	3,239	.478	.863	895	451	1,741	21.2
81–82	Boston	77	2,923	.503	.863	837	447	1,761	22.9
82–83	Boston	79	2,982	.504	.840	870	458	1,867	23.6
83–84	Boston	79	3,028	.492	.888	796	520	1,908	24.2
84–85	Boston	80	3,161	.522	.882	842	531	2,295	28.7
85–86	Boston	82	3,113	.496	.896	805	557	2,115	25.8
86–87	Boston	74	3,005	.525	.910	682	566	2,076	28.1
87–88	Boston	76	2,965	.527	.916	703	467	2,275	29.9
88–89	Boston	6	189	.471	.947	37	29	116	19.3
89–90	Boston	75	2,944	.473	.930	712	562	1,820	24.3
90–91	Boston	60	2,277	.454	.891	509	431	1,164	19.4
91–92	Boston	45	1,662	.466	.926	434	306	908	20.2
TOTALS		897	34,443	.496	.886	8,974	5,695	21,791	24.3

NBA PLAYOFF RECORD

SEASON	TEAM	G	MIN	FG PCT	FT PCT	REB	AST	PTS	AVG
79–80	Boston	9	372	.469	.880	101	42	192	21.3
80–81	Boston	17	750	.470	.894	238	103	373	21.9
81–82	Boston	12	490	.427	.822	150	67	214	17.8
82–83	Boston	6	240	.422	.828	75	41	123	20.5
83–84	Boston	23	961	.524	.879	252	136	632	27.5
84–85	Boston	20	815	.461	.890	182	115	520	26.0
85–86	Boston	18	770	.517	.927	168	148	466	25.9
86–87	Boston	23	1,015	.476	.912	231	165	622	27.0
87–88	Boston	17	763	.450	.894	150	115	417	24.5
89–90	Boston	5	207	.444	.906	46	44	122	24.4
90–91	Boston	10	396	.408	.863	72	65	171	17.1
91–92	Boston	4	107	.500	.750	18	21	45	11.3
TOTALS		164	6,886	.472	.890	1,683	1,062	3,897	23.8

NBA ALL-STAR GAME RECORD

SEASON	TEAM	MIN	FG PCT	FT PCT	REB	AST	PTS
1980	Boston	23	.500	—	6	7	7
1981	Boston	18	.200	—	4	3	2
1982	Boston	28	.583	.625	12	5	19
1983	Boston	29	.500	—	13	7	14
1984	Boston	33	.333	1.000	7	3	16
1985	Boston	31	.500	.833	8	2	21
1986	Boston	35	.444	.833	8	5	23
1987	Boston	35	.389	1.000	6	5	18
1988	Boston	32	.250	1.000	7	1	6
1990	Boston	23	.375	1.000	8	3	8
1991	Boston		Did not play — injured				
1992	Boston		Did not play — injured				
TOTALS		287	.423	.844	79	41	134

David ROBINSON

Although David Robinson is one of the most agile centers ever to play basketball, he brings much more than agility to his team. His courage and coolheaded approach have helped him become the finest defensive player in the game. And his quiet confidence and thoughtful character have made him a leader on every team he has played for.

At 7'1", David can leap as high on the boards as anyone in the NBA, but his ability to anticipate the moves of opposing players is the key to his defense. He led the league in steals and blocked shots in the 1991–92 season, and is such a powerful presence on the court that an opposing player will often hesitate to come near him, fearing he'll see his shot slapped back in his face. David has been compared to Bill Russell, the great center of the Boston Celtics, the champion team of the 1950s and '60s.

David was born August 6, 1965, in Key West, Florida, but he grew up in Virginia Beach, Virginia, where his father, Ambrose, was in the Navy. Ambrose was often away from the family for many weeks at a time, but when he was home he spent as much time as he could with his family.

David was an avid reader and also loved playing the piano and programming computers. Math was David's favorite subject, and from the time he was small he could add long columns of numbers in his head. When David was 15, his father went away to sea for a month. David decided to surprise him by building a video projection screen from a kit. When Ambrose returned home, he was treated to his favorite TV show on a 6-foot screen!

David is often able to block the shooter's view of the basket. And even though he isn't credited by the scorer with a blocked shot, he has still prevented the score.

David didn't have basketball shoes, so when he arrived he took his street shoes off. Someone passed him the ball and shouted, ''Now let's see you dunk!'' In bare feet David flew into the air, swooped over the basket, and drove the ball through! It didn't take the coach long to decide that there was room on the team for David.

The day after David made the team, the starting center went down with an injury. David took over and played well, although he was far from dominant.

Although there was a high school near his home, David rode a bus to a smaller school thirteen miles away. He didn't know anyone at this school, but it didn't take him long to realize that because there were fewer athletes in the school he had a good chance of making the varsity sports teams.

He began his first year late, and the basketball coach had already made final cuts from the roster. But David was 6′7″ and very athletic, and when the coach saw him on the basketball court, he asked him to come to practice that afternoon.

Despite his many blocks, David never fouled out of a game in high school, and he hit often with an accurate left-handed bank shot.

David scored over 1300 on his college board exams and was recruited by a number of schools, including several in the Ivy League. After talking it over with his family, David decided to attend the Naval Academy at Annapolis. The Academy was close to him, and he liked knowing that he was assured of a job as a naval officer. His father reminded him that he might not want to commit to five years of military service after graduation, but David held firm.

David's experience at Navy was not what he'd expected. Wherever the first-year ''plebes'' went, older students gave orders, taunts, and abuse. Plebes were forbidden to have radios, watch TV, or leave the yard except between noon and midnight on Saturday. Reveille (wakeup call) was at 5 A.M., and students had three hours of military drill every day.

Like all the other students, David found it difficult, but he knew that if he focused on basketball and studying his work would be rewarded. And he was able to escape most of the harassment because of his size and strong character.

By the end of his freshman season, David was a basketball star. He had chosen Navy for its academics and the security of a job afterward, but was rapidly becoming a great attraction on the basketball court.

'TEN-HUT!!

In 1986 David was among NCAA leaders in scoring and rebounding, and he blocked more shots than all but one team in the country!

Now he had to face the most difficult choice of his life. He could transfer to a school like Georgetown or Kentucky, where he could concentrate on basketball. From there he might possibly move on to the NBA, where he could make millions. Or he could choose to stay at the Academy, concentrate on his studies in electronics, and fulfill the Navy requirement of five years of military service after graduation.

After a long talk with his father and uncle, who laid out the pros and cons of both choices, David had to make up his mind.

David knew that if he transferred he would have to sit out a year, which at that stage in his development could be very harmful. He also felt that money wasn't the most important thing: "A lot of people," he later said, "think you are automatically happy if you have a lot of money. I don't necessarily think that's true."

David decided to stay at Navy. That summer he tried to cram his huge frame into a 6-foot berth on a submarine and went through a tough Marine boot camp. In the fall he tried out for a U.S. college team that traveled through Europe, and saw the level of intensity that other star college players brought to the game. Five months later, led by David, Navy went to the NCAA Final Eight before losing to Duke.

David had grown close to 7 feet tall, and his thoughts were more and more on the pros. That summer he was released from Navy assignment to join the U.S. team at the World Championships. The team reached the final game and took a 78–60 lead into the last 8 minutes, then held off the Soviets to win, 87–85, the first U.S. world title since 1954.

In his senior year David became frustrated at being kept away from basketball by the Academy routine, which demanded that everyone maintain the same schedule. Even so, he starred in game after game, drawing raves in Kentucky for a 45-point, 14-rebound, 10-block masterpiece. He won one game with a 17-foot hook in the last second and another with a 40-foot bank shot at the buzzer.

David became the first player in NCAA history to score 2,500 points and 1,300 rebounds; as a senior he averaged 28.2 points per game and was chosen College Player of the Year. He holds thirty-three Naval Academy records and three NCAA records, including 14 blocked shots in one game.

David was the first pick in the 1987 draft lottery and signed with San Antonio. Because of his size, he was commissioned by the Navy as a "restricted line officer" after graduation, and his stint was shortened to two years. Rumors began to spread in San Antonio that he'd arrive even sooner, and thousands of season tickets were immediately snapped up. Before he'd even played a game, David had helped save a franchise where attendance had been down.

In discussions at the Academy, David had been led to believe that he'd be able to defer part of his service in order to turn pro after the 1988 Olympics. But in the spring of 1987 a new Secretary of the Navy insisted that he serve the full two years, plus six years of reserve duty in the off-season. Although the decision upset fans in San Antonio, David accepted it in stride. He would play in the Olympics, then try to keep in good basketball form while the Spurs struggled through another season without him.

David was finally able to join San Antonio in July of 1989, and he immediately revitalized the team. Since his arrival in the NBA he's averaged 24 points and 12 rebounds a game, and has starred in the All-Star Game each year. In David's rookie season, Isiah Thomas proclaimed Robinson "the player of the '90s," and all signs indicate Isiah was right.

In his last college game, David scored 50 points against Michigan in the NCAA playoffs, one of the greatest performances in tournament history.